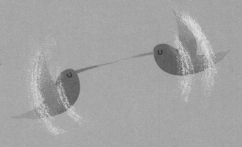

For Zoë – I really, really
love you, Zo!
~ K N

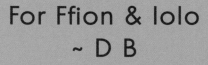

For Ffion & Iolo
~ D B

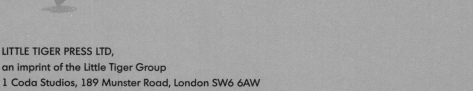

LITTLE TIGER PRESS LTD,
an imprint of the Little Tiger Group
1 Coda Studios, 189 Munster Road, London SW6 6AW
Imported into the EEA by Penguin Random House Ireland,
Morrison Chambers, 32 Nassau Street, Dublin D02 YH68
www.littletiger.co.uk

First published in Great Britain 2023

Text copyright © Karl Newson 2023
Illustrations copyright © Duncan Beedie 2023
Karl Newson and Duncan Beedie have asserted their rights
to be identified as the author and illustrator of this work
under the Copyright, Designs and Patents Act, 1988
A CIP catalogue record for this book is available
from the British Library
All rights reserved • ISBN 978-1-80104-408-0

Printed in China • LTP/2800/4805/0622

10 9 8 7 6 5 4 3 2 1

The Forest Stewardship Council® (FSC®) is an international,
non-governmental organisation dedicated to promoting
responsible management of the world's forests. FSC®
operates a system of forest certification and product
labelling that allows consumers to identify wood and
wood-based products from well-managed forests.

For more information about the FSC®, please visit their
website at www.fsc.org

FSC
www.fsc.org
MIX
Paper from
responsible sources
FSC® C017606

This Little Tiger book belongs to:

_____

_____

_____

I REALLY REALLY LOVE YOU SO

KARL NEWSON

LITTLE TIGER
LONDON

DUNCAN BEEDIE

I really, really, really, really,
REALLY LOVE YOU SO!

I thought that I should tell you,
just in case you didn't know . . .

Nothing is as lovely as a **great big hug** with you!

I really, really **love** you so.

I do.

I do.

I
DO!

I'd like to find a special way
to show the **love in me** . . .
I'll wrestle with a crocodile!

I'll sail out to **sea!**

No . . .

. . . I'll climb the **tallest** mountain and I'll write it in the

snow!

It's really, really, really, **REALLY COLD** UP HERE you know!

Maybe you'd prefer a bunch of

flowers?

Or a stick?

Maybe I could find a **hat** and do a **magic** trick?!

Maybe

I could make you

something

special,

like a card?

Or a robot?

Or a **rocket?!**

WHY

IS

MAKING

THINGS

SO HARD?!

I really, really, really,
really, really–

KANGAROO!

Aha!

I'll watch the **other animals** and **copy** what they do!

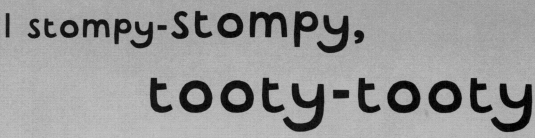

I stompy-**Stompy**,
tooty-tooty
really love you so!

I love you from **my bottom** to the **top** of every tree!

I love you

when I'm running

while a **bear** is

chasing me!

I love you
when I'm hiding
and **I love**
you when–

*"They went the
other way
from here!"*

OH DEAR!

It's time for **a disguise** . . .

PHEW.

I love you when I'm tired
and I love you grumpy, too!

I love you when you're snoring like a lion (like you do) . . .

Love is like a **sparkle** and a **twinkle** in my toes . . .

And it **tingles** up my **tummy** . . .

It snorts inside
my nose . . .

And I thought that I should tell you,
just in case you didn't know . . .

. . . I really, really, really, **really,** REALLY

LOVE

YOU SO!

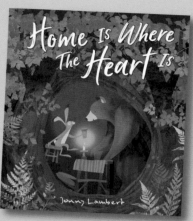
Home Is Where The Heart Is
Jonny Lambert

CAPTAIN CUDDLES
MAGGIE POWELL-TUCK
JULIO ANTONIO BLASCO
SAVING THE WORLD ONE HUG AT A TIME!

THE FAIRY DOGMOTHER
Caroline Crowe · Richard Merritt

I Love You More than All the Stars
Becky Davies · Dana Brown

More heartwarming stories to fall in love with . . .

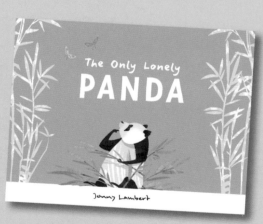
The Only Lonely PANDA
Jonny Lambert

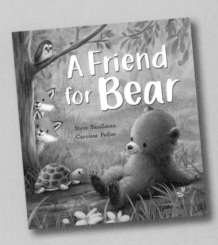
A Friend for Bear
Steve Smallman · Caroline Pedler

LITTLE TIGER

For information regarding any of the above titles or for our catalogue, please contact us: Little Tiger Press Ltd, 1 Coda Studios, 189 Munster Road, London SW6 6AW • Tel: 020 7385 6333
E-mail: contact@littletiger.co.uk • www.littletiger.co.uk